J. R. McRae

Free Passage

Illustrated by
Terry Hand

First edition, USA, 2013
Second edition, first published in Australia by Word Wings in 2016.

Second edition, first Australian edition 2016.

Designed by Terry Hand

National Library of Australia Cataloguing-in-Publication entry

Creator: McRae, J. R., author.

Title: Free passage / J.R. McRae;
Illustrator, designer Terence "Terry" Hand.

ISBN: 9781925484113 (paperback)

Subjects: Slavery--Fiction.
Immigrants--Fiction.
Orphans--Fiction.
War and families--Fiction.
Disabilities--Fiction.
War stories.
United States--History--Civil War, 1861-1865--Fiction.

Other Creators/Contributors:
Hand, Terence, illustrator.

Dewey Number: A823.3

Contents

I wish to acknowledge and thank Jan Turner-Jones, Wendy Brealey, Jane Greenwood, Madeline Sharples, Matthew Anderson and David Grugeon for their editorial and proofreading assistance.

And I would also like to thank Terry Hand for his very helpful suggestions and all his perseverence and patience as we ploughed through the edits and alterations long-distance.

Dedicated to my five children and husband Geoff. Thank you all for your support.

JRP

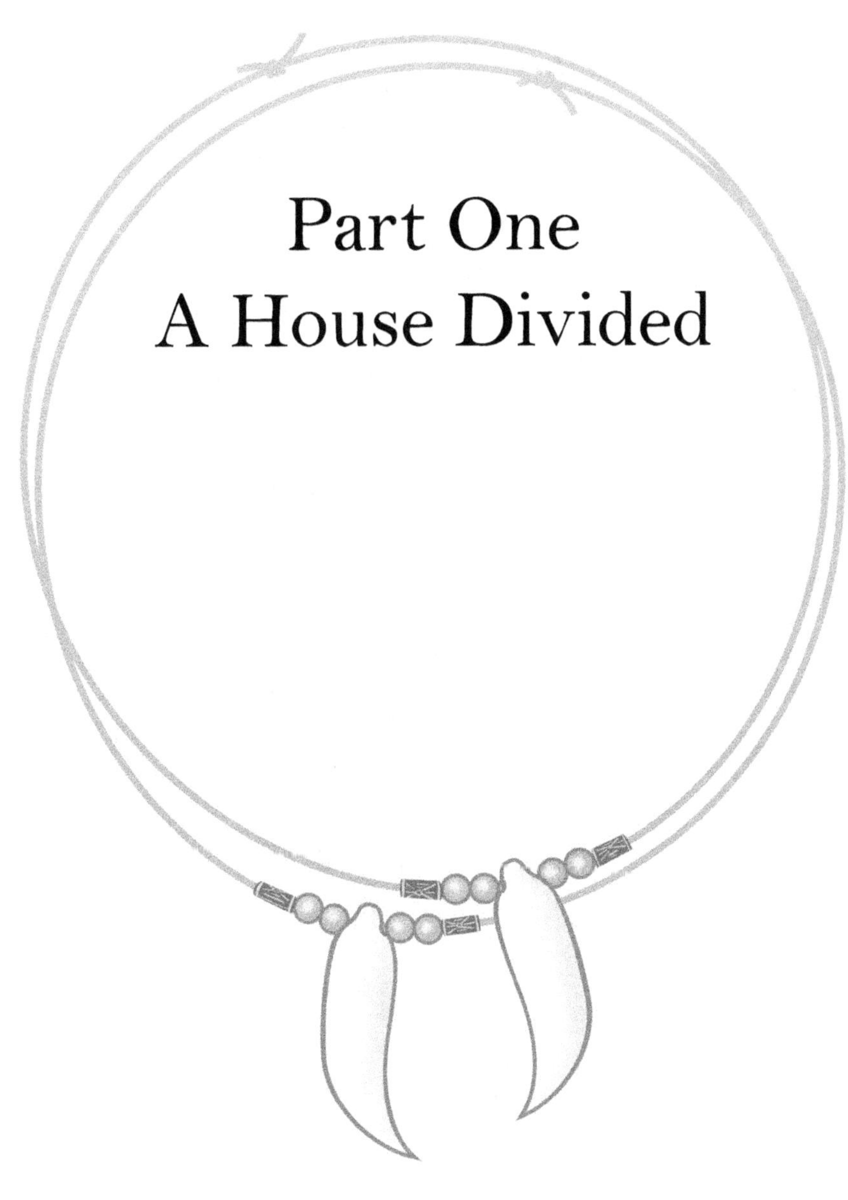

Part One
A House Divided

The mood of the court shifted slightly as Dane entered under escort. Servicemen whispered behind gloved hands. The General sat po-faced, looking straight ahead.

Dane's uniform, showing signs of battle fatigue, had been pressed. His medal gleamed on his chest in all its untarnished glory… He passed under the lamplight to what served as a dock, the medal flashed. This did not escape the General's notice. He winced. Just days ago, he had pinned it on Dane's chest.

Court martial, summary court martial and execution for a hero who walked out on a battle, the General almost imperceptibly shook his head.

A career soldier, Dane had no qualms about killing. Soldiers did that. A good soldier gave his all! He'd been mentioned in dispatches. How many times? The General tried to recall but lost count. Bravery under fire, distinguished service, he knew how to rally his men to give their best. Dane set the agenda, no risk too great, if his men's lives were at stake, if the advantage could be taken, ground won. A soldier's soldier, born leader, what went wrong?

Dane had done the unforgivable. In the heat of battle, he had turned and simply walked. A stray bullet glanced off his epaulet - that was it, like he was charmed.

Under the shocked gaze of a speechless commander, Dane passed through the ranks of his men and kept walking till the noise of fire dulled. He walked into the command tent and surrendered his commission. Just like that.

Dane always led, the angry, driven adventurer. Paul followed his older twin into whatever hell he led them. Paul followed, role undefined, his person malleable, just go where Dane led.

Out on the lake in their uncle's skiff, a storm hit. Both near drowned. Dane, ringleader, was lashed till he bled. It did nothing to deter him. Paul was forced to witness as his lesson. Dane's eyes never blinked.

He took Paul hunting with their father's rifles. Dane wanted bear. They found it, ranging in the North Kentucky woods back of the ranch. The bear turned and fair galloped at them. Dane shoved Paul ahead around a tree, twisted and shot the bear through the heart as it reared to strike. Its dying, blood-warm breath burst over them in the sigh of wind at winter's end. It fell and shuddered earth and rock.

Dane took the great incisors. One for him, one for Paul, round their necks on leather he cured himself from its hide. The skin, head intact, carpeted their shared sleeping quarters.

There had been no punishment that time. The bear had taken cattle.

That winter the unthinkable happened. "There's no help George," their mother's voice, despairing, drifted upstairs.

"I know Jessica, I know," their father, annoyed, resigned,

"there 's no one else with your Pa gone. Damn your sister."

"George!" their mother's voice ricocheted with shock off the stone walls of the ranch house.

"Damn, Jessica! We need you, and what's your sister do, run off with a no good soldier boy. Gets herself taken in the territories. He gets a medal she gets scalped and how's that help now?"

The boys could hear their mother softly crying. "She needs me…"

Their father cut her short. "She had the lot! Servants, everything and your no good Pa!" The boys knew the streams of money trickled off East to Richmond, Virginia, to pay Pa's gambling debts, keep food on the table. Not enough for their grandmother's lifestyle, too much for her idle, flighty mind. Her demands became wilder, increased till their father refused another cent. A month gone, Pa was found with a bullet in his brain. The magistrate had contacted them. He had placed Grandmother in an asylum. Father had read the letter at the dinner table. Their mother, humiliated, sobbing softly, her head hanging down on her bosom, made no comment.

"For her own good, he says." Their father sighed, "For her own damn good. Woman needed a hiding long gone!" Their mother's sobs loudened.

"STOP sniveling woman!" Father put down the letter and thumped his fists onto the table so the crockery jumped. "What in tarnation do you expect ME to do?"

Their mother, as usual, said nothing. The usual silent warfare ensued over the following months, broken by bouts of swearing when their father lost patience.

Silence wore him down.

The first snows arrived, chill with their mother and Paul's departure. "It won't," her voice trembled, "won't be long, George, her health has never been good, you know that.

Paul will do well out there. They have fine colleges, a fine university. I need him, need someone, I…" Father's impatient kiss shut her up.

Mother hugged Dane till he pushed her off. Ranch hands watching, sniggering behind their hands. "I'm right, Mother! Paul will see to you, right, brother?"

The boys clapped each other on the back. The younger, gentler twin, Paul's eyes misted. Dane didn't trust himself to speak.

He stood watching the distant train lights long after his father had mounted up the dray and left with the order, "Expect you in the hour. No later."

When even the imaginary echo of wheels on steel track had faded, Dane mounted and took his time back.

Without his mother and Paul's peacekeeping, Dane grew angrier, picked fights with the men, gave as good as he got and maintained a sullen silence round his father.

Letters arrived. They brought no comfort.

"She is putting on weight and so happy to see us! It is lovely. Folk are so refined. It's just like old times. The place is looking like a new pin! Mind, we only live on the bottom storey. We don't need more. Sissy Becker's housekeeper has a simple girl. The girl comes twice a week. You have to yell at her with EVERYTHING, but she works hard." There was no mention of home.

Paul's letter to Dane told a different story. "We might as well be home. You know Grandmother treats Mother like Father always did. Demand, demand from sun up to sun down. God I'm glad I'm no woman. I'd like to take Mother away. The old lady's killing her. She sits and gets fat and gives orders and there's just Mother and Girl. Funny, no one gives her a name, just 'Girl'. Girl goes home at dusk and Mother has to cope till I get home from college. I swear Grandmother's like caring for a big baby. It's getting worse. She won't get around and her legs are seizing up. Doctor told her as much but she has this sick, sly grin like she knows exactly what she's doing. Miss you, brother. Try and write."

Father sat by the fire holding Mother's letter, staring into the flames. Then he stood up, threw it in and stormed out. He spent the night in town. Next day, when he returned, he smelled of strange perfume.

Letter after letter came with no mention of an end date. Father's visits to town increased.

The letters from Mother came less often, the stay more entrenched.

"My Mother is so in need, so frail. George, it is so sad. She needs me so much. I'm all she has poor pet. I think Girl isn't simple, she understands well enough when she's looking at your lips, even though she says naught but a cry if Grandmother strikes at her with the walking stick. She seems to be honest though. I have offered her to stay upstairs. I really need her here. My Mother is getting heavy. We could do with Dane's strong arms, but there, you need him."

Paul still wrote as regular but the longing for home dimmed. There was distraction. "I swear, brother, I never thought I'd call one of our own ugly. Grandmother's ugly. There I've said it. She has a meanness and a cunning and her temper is something to see. She has broken so much crockery we are now using the remnants of the best dinner service. I told Mother we should serve her on enamelware but she will have none of it. Only the best for her mama! Girl is my comfort. She stays here now. She's not simple, part deaf and mute's all. I've been teaching her. She can cipher and read now and her writing is fair. Don't speak of this to anyone."

Looking out the bay window in the direction of town, Dane considered heading east. Then, with the thought of the woman-dominated house, he shook his head. Women! Father's outbursts had subsided somewhat but the common talk had it he 'kept a woman' in town. As Dane watched, a dust cloud moved along the road from town. Visitors were few. He fixed his gaze till he recognized his father's surrey and pair. He started to turn when a figure on the seat next to his father caught his attention. A woman, why was father bringing her here – a housekeeper? Too young, clothing too fine, father's fancy woman! He started back as the realization hit. A whore! His father dared bring home his whore!

Dane headed for his quarters and threw essentials in his duffle bag. Rumblings of war had been about. He had thought to enlist. The whore decided things. The new rifle with the sights, Father's toy, Dane lifted it from its case in Father's study and was saddling up on his father's prize black stallion as the surrey pulled up to the front of the house. He headed up the back road, north, and didn't look back. As he cleared the property line, he heard a distant roar and smiled. Father missed the horse and rifle, not the son.

Soldiering suited Dane neat as the fit of his uniform. Months passed in march time. Officer material was on short supply and he wrote the textbook. They kept on the move, town-to-town, bivouac in forest, in field, mud, slush and spring green. One more letter arrived from Paul, part torn, mud spattered. The postmark told of many months' travel.

"Well you sure did it this time brother, Father is mad as hell! Can't blame you though. Word has it there is a housekeeper at the spread now, young, pretty. Mother is none too happy but she won't leave Grandmother. Pity.

I have my own concerns. Girl and I want to marry. No one will wed us here. Girl is what folks call mulatto. Before you react, think of Father's half-caste brother, Pelletier, by his father's wilderness wife, remember, the trapper from beyond the Great Lakes. He was good to us that one time he came. I've written to him. Girl and I want to head to Canada. They will marry us there. Mother is worn down by Grandmother. She may not last as long as her own mother. But I cannot wait. They are conscripting all able-bodied men here, even those in dotage and boys. If I don't leave now with Girl, my own family goes unprotected. You read aright. Girl is with child. We've hidden it best we can. Mother would throw Girl out on principle. Grandmother would have an apoplexy. We must go now best we can and make Canada by autumn. Finding Pelletier may take time, something we don't have. By the time you get this I hope to be gone. If you can, come, please come for Mother's sake."

Dane wrote a few scant words of letter in return. He stuffed both in his coat pocket, threw his rifle over his shoulder and headed out to his men.

The sky was turning. The long shadows reached down the mountain, invading the valley plain.

All day, Dane had rallied his men in the thick of fire with the ferocity of those trained and consecrated to the arts of war. Sweat and blood ran in rivulets down the creases of his face. He licked at the corners of his mouth, salt sweet and warm, a slightly meaty, sickly taste. His or that of the newly dead trod under his boots, blood's blood. He looked in the eyes of men he fought, unafraid to know his enemy. Others of his men flinched at this. Young Jenkins, Bible Joe, Gramps Elshaw, conscripts, grit teeth soldiers fighting for their homes and families, these men shied from carrying the burden of that recognition, that moment when the man confronting you knows he has met his fate. They killed like desperate boys in the schoolyard, clenching eyes and flailing fists.

The day covered with blood, soaked the horizon long red… The ground stamped to mud. What grass there was, blood caked and rocks spattered. Any moment, the generals would sound retreat for the night and bivouac, gather their dead and injured whilst there was still light to identify the uniform.

For Dane, days ended half finished, work lying in the cradle of the gun undone. Blood hunger, addictive restlessness, Dane drove them stumbling tired into the very teeth of the enemy, calling and cursing them on. They were nearing the Confederacy eastern stronghold. Men fought with renewed vigour an enemy flagging and worn.

"We're damned," Bible Joe would mutter in his prayers before battle, "God help us."

At day's wane, he rallied his men, one last time. A farm boy with red hair, one of his new recruits fell gashed open in front of him. "Bastard!" Dane fired at the soldier who turned, blood still dripping from his bayonet. The man looked up in Dane's eyes as he fell. Recognition…

The house was quiet in the lull of afternoon. Grandmother snored noisily and Mother had collapsed into the sleep of soul-weary exhaustion. Up the staircase Paul and Girl had everything prepared weeks before, awaiting such an opportunity. The donkey was tethered in the trees. Horses and livestock confiscated months before for the war effort.

Again and again their escape had been thwarted. Mother would force herself awake like a frightened young wife over her first born, watching the heave and fall of Grandmother's chest. She would sleep, finally. They would pull their things together fast, only to have Grandmother wake with yelled demands and throw the house into chaos.

Time had elapsed. The war crept perilously closer, closer. Yesterday, the local guard had started door to door conscription of all the able bodied and many not so. Today must be it.

Bags slung over shoulder, they reached the top of the great staircase. They were going down to the pantry to gather the last of their journey's supplies. Girl glanced out through the huge windows that looked down the gentle valley to town. The dust of horsemen caught her eye. Her fingers dug urgently into Paul's arm. He followed her gaze and pulled her swiftly back to the rear of the house. No taking the stairs now. Sheets tore off beds and strung together in a makeshift rope. As he lowered Girl down with most supplies, she looked up. Loud as he dared, he said, "Head into the woods. I'll follow. If anything happens, keep going to Canada." She nodded as she bumped to the ground, scrambled up and headed to the trees. The slope was wet with a rain shower. Girl slipped, tried to protect a belly not yet noticeable to any but the most astute. A sharp cry! Her foot twisted under her. She looked helplessly up at Paul and tried to drag herself to the trees.

From the house two sounds mingled, Grandmother's yell for attention and a thunderous knocking at the door. Paul shimmied down the sheets, hurled the makeshift rope out of sight and headed to Girl as the sound of horse hooves made him turn.

Next instant, he was under guard. He and the girl were dragged unceremoniously round to the front door, where her Grandmother waited, rage in every self-indulgent line of her face. "Ma'am, you need to keep a better reign on your darkie here. Headed to the woods and him after her." The laugh was dirty and Grandmother missed none of the implications. The

barrage of language woke Mother who stumbled in disheveled and shrank back with embarrassment at the assembled group that greeted her.

Mother, to her credit, pleaded eloquently for Paul's release. "Pity, good sir! We have no man but my son to run this place. As you see, we are women and one an invalid. We..."

"You've darkie here! More than many with the wretches running north like hares before hounds. The Confederacy needs him more!" With that he turned on his heel and his men pulled Paul after them.

Paul's eyes met Girl's. "Trapper." And that was it.

The march into town took eternity with Mother's cries still ringing in his ears and Grandmother's curses. Stronger was Girl's look. At least, he knew, first opportunity she would go north. First chance, he would too.

Basic training amounted to the question, "Can you shoot?" The uniform was ill fitting and had a bullet wound in the coat as must have finished the previous occupant. He was herded north. First he knew of battle was the sound, bullets, canon, cries of the defiant and the dying.

He did what he had done all his life. Followed. He fired, ran, fired mechanically. Didn't dare look at the dead and dying in case he recognized what no man wants to see, his own fate staring back. The coat, spattered beyond recognition now, bore red badges of courage and mud, caked thick.

Ahead was a pack of them charging down in a fury of blades and fire. The officer out front a blur of blue and blood. Then it was all around him.

One moment, a red-haired country boy was charging him bayonet fixed, next he was twisting on the ground beside Paul, his guts spilling. Paul fired again. The body stilled. He swerved front to see the muzzle of the officer's gun discharge. The blue sky blackened over him, a blanket.

In the confusion at sunset, his body was gathered up with Union fallen and laid out with their dead.

"Sir!"

"At ease Sergeant." Lucas had the impatient edge of a man with other things on his mind, "What is it?"

"One of the dead men, sir. The boys thought it Dane and brought it in. Uncanny alike. The bear tooth and the uniform so matted it could've been Union. But it ain't Dane, sir?"

"Show me!"

They strode through lines of dead and wounded to a body whose barely recognizable coat in the half-light, bore two bullet holes, one old, one fresh with blood.

Lucas bent over and took the bear tooth with its thong of hide, clenching it in his fist.

"Take it back man. Some mother needs to know her boy is gone."

He stood staring at the dead man till the Sergeant commandeered orderlies to carry the body over. Dane had mentioned an incident ... A truth dawned, awful in its realization.

"You know it's the firing squad," The General looked back at Dane's commanding officer, Major Lucas, addressing him with more than a hint of concern in his voice.

The court had adjourned. Guilty.

"We found letters in his keeping. One from Confederate territory asking his help. One from Dane himself, short but no mistaking, 'I'm coming, God willing, I'm coming.' The General's face and voice gave no ground.

Lucas tried again, matter-of-fact as he could, "It's

thought the letter was from his twin out East."

"'A house divided against itself shall fall', Mark 3, verse 25." The General coughed. The anomaly of the medal, citations, had not sat well with him. The man was an example. He must be an example now.

Lucas noted the set of the General's jaw. No mercy there. Dane had followed Lucas up through the ranks. Try as he might to keep professional distance, this angry young man impressed him, no less because of his own troubled background.

The execution had been set for sun up. Lucas went to the enclosure that served as stockade. Dane stood alone, hands tied. Lucas looked over his shoulder to the tether lines where Dane's black stallion grazed a few scant feet away.

The shadows were long on the ground and dark winging in on clouds. What were the chances? Lucas wandered over to the stallion and patted his neck. Casually he slipped the tether. As dark swept in, Lucas relieved a grateful sentry, hunched over with tiredness at his post, and eased himself quietly into the stockade.

Dane registered surprise but said nothing. Lucas reached out and took the bear tooth round Dane's neck in his hand, holding up the other as he did. In the last glimmer of light, it was obvious. "Your twin. Why say nothing?" He pressed the tooth into Dane's hand.

"I shot him. Just firing into enemy. There he was dying in front of me and me it was pulled the trigger. My brother."

Lucas shook his head, "The letters, Girl, the babe have no one now. Do this for your brother." He glanced around, "The stallion's untethered. Go."

Dane stole through the dark shadows, a few strides and he was mounted and off heading north.

The General sat at his campfire musing at the dark.

Something flickered at the edge of his vision - a medal on a chest, the black stallion full gallop.

"Marksman!" The General's arm swung unmistakably in the direction of the fleeing horse. The sentry fired. The rider shuddered and fell. The horse rode on.

Ashen faced, Lucas stared at the General. "Fetch the body, Lucas. You've saved us bullets."

Lucas strode the short distance to where he knew the body lay, barely visible in the dark. He bent down. Blood trickled from Dane's mouth but he was still alive. "Take these, for Girl." His useless right hand held the one, his left hand struggled with the tooth around his own neck and went limp. Lucas pocketed both and closed the dead eyes. If humanly possible, if he survived long enough, he'd deliver.

Girl was trying to help Grandmother onto the commode the day the officer came to the door. Paul had been gone scarcely more than a month.

Mother cried out to Girl to answer the door. Grandmother yelled back, "Answer yourself, you sniveling ninny! Girl is doing for ME!"

Mother's gown rustled, all agitation as she hurried to the door, lifted the latch with shaking hands and let the door creak back on aching hinges.

Back in the privy, Girl, now having more difficulty hiding her condition, was struggling to seat the heavy, old woman.

"HURRY UP! Stupid mute! HURRY UP! If I shit myself you'll wear it!"

Girl stifled a sigh, knowing Mother would be blushing with embarrassment as this last pronouncement thundered down the corridor.

Mother's voice shook at the import of a uniformed man at her door, "Good day, officer, what might be the reason for your visit? As you see we are women alone, defenseless. My son..."

The officer, uncomfortable with his duty, interrupted, "Your son, Ma'am, he died in..."

His voice trailed off as Mother screamed and fell at his feet, letters and a small parcel fell from her pocket.

In the back room, Girl sensed more than heard and ran. She knelt by the ashen woman and looked up at the officer.

His muttered, "In the line of duty..." was drowned by abusive yells from the privy.

Tears trickling down her face she held Mother's hand. She was too still. The officer put his head on her chest then his cheek up to her nose and lips.

He looked into Girl's eyes, his voice kind for a southerner, "Gone, miss," He lifted Mother's prone form and placed her on the settee. He paused, took Girl's chin, "Sorrow for your mistress does you credit, my girl. Don't worry. I'll fetch the doctor. You'll need a certificate."

She nodded and looked over her shoulder to the backroom from where Grandmother's high pitched invective spewed down to them in a volatile stream.

The officer, stood, bowed and turned to leave, nearly slipping on the fallen letters.

He handed them and the parcel to Girl, glancing at the top letter as he did, "No, wonder, poor woman..."

When had it come, that morning? Girl's eyes flicked across the polite, but coldly official words, 'We regret...' So Dane too was gone. The second letter, more personal, was from an officer called Lucas. The words within would stop any mother's heart. The final letters were the brothers' last correspondence. Girl clutched them to her belly, sending up a silent prayer for her unborn boy, she knew it was a boy, she even knew his name, Paulie, 'God don't let our son… Please God, never Paulie!' Her fingers shook as she undid the little parcel – two bear teeth on identical leather thongs fell out and landed at her feet.

Renewed screams of abuse from the closet brought her back with a jolt. Her own grief would have to wait. She stuffed the letters and the bear's teeth in her pinafore. These would not matter to the old witch; they did matter to her. One day, they would matter to Paulie.

Girl hurried, reluctantly, to attend to the yells. She struggled with Grandmother, ducking the old woman's flailing efforts to hit her with the walking stick.

The rest of the day was a nightmare of waiting, trying to deal with Grandmother's demands. She seemed to have no idea what had happened to her grandsons nor a care for her daughter beyond demands to know why Mother was not carrying out her filial duty. The doctor's arrival did not make things easier.

He pronounced Mother dead and told Grandmother he would send the undertaker. He knew the family plot, he said, and asked if arrangements had been made for Paul's body to be moved there.

"Well do it man! I'm a sick woman and all I have is this dumb idiot's care. What are you gawking at you ignorant darkie! Make tea for the doctor and me!"

"No, Ma'am, thank you. I'd best be off, making arrangements." He nodded to Girl, "I'll let myself out!"

Alone at last, Girl rubbed her lower back. She tried to make dinner in between running backwards and forwards to meet the old woman's incessant, shouted demands.

That night, Girl let her emotions loose into the pillow. Paul's last word to her echoed around her mind as she drifted asleep. It was still night when she stirred. The candle still flicked hope in the dark room. Her mind crowded with thoughts. She knew Paul wanted her to take their child and head to freedom. Not just survive, but live free, looking every man and woman in the eye with her head up. He would still want this.

She had kept what they packed tucked under her bed. Grandmother's snores drifted up, loud under the influence of her sleeping draught. Girl got out the bundles and added more things for the baby. She had taken to binding her stomach part to hide, part to protect, these last weeks. She must go. War was on their doorstep. The Confederacy ingloriously losing.

How long would her journey take? She poured over an old map by candlelight, traced her fingers over the route north. She remembered the last known address for Pelletier. She wrote, a letter to Pelletier and a note for the undertaker. During his visit tomorrow, perhaps she could prevail upon his kindness, perhaps... a desperate hope. And there was still the donkey. She must go.

The old woman would argue over every arrangement, would drive the undertaker to distraction, would take time. Family pride and two bodies demanded this. Time, precious time, Girl needed.

Girl checked everything twice before finally snuffing her candle and falling back asleep.

The morning came with driving rain. Grandmother, louder than ever, swore and blamed, swung at her with the stick. The hours crawled past. Girl didn't hear till the undertaker's polite knock became an insistent banging. The thin man under the towering black umbrella looked as though he wanted to shelter all the bereaved under its black bat wings.

"Morning, Miss. Is Madame Ingenuie Dubonnet in?"

Girl looked at him blankly till the man repeated himself to her face, but louder. Blushing with embarrassment she signalled him in. She had not heard Grandmother called by her name in years.

Grandmother's barked greeting, "You're late!" roared up the stairs after Girl as she left them to sort their grim business.

The rain drummed incessantly on the tiles. Her plans drowned in the widening puddles on the tiled landing at the top of the stone steps up from the lower carriage path. The steps were more decorative than serving any practical purpose. The carriage path made a circular drive right up to the entrance porch.

Her heart hammering in her ears, Girl descended with her things and sequestered them out back. The man who'd sensed her hardness of hearing, bellowed, "I'll let myself out, Miss!"

Girl hurried up but not before Grandmother let fly an invective that made the dour man blush. Taking advantage of his discomfort, Girl handed him her letter and the note, 'For the late woman's son, would you, sir, kindly post this?'

He read, nodded and left.

The undertaker would do what he did best, undertake – the coffins, the preacher, the funeral details, the hearse, even the flowers. It would be no sooner than the end of the week. Too long. The Union frontrunners could be upon them any time. Despite the Union abolitionist claims, many Unionists were as anti runaways as southerners. Confederate men on the run from the field were ragged, hungry and often enough, dangerous. She would work her way north where she could, while she could. It would be a long journey.

Overnight, the rain eased. By early morning the grey was lifting and the rain stopped. The ground was sodden.

Before sunrise, Girl woke and prepared. She crept downstairs and swallowed a hurried breakfast. The old woman snored loudly. Girl made a last minute decision to take Mother's good, heavy, old winter coat. It was big enough that it would warm her when her belly swelled its fullest but it was much too small for Grandmother. She knew Mother would have given it to her with a caution - 'don't you let Grandmother know, you hear now!' - the way she had passed many things to Girl over the years. She took it off its hook and threw it on, for convenience.

Girl headed down, and was making her way to the cupboard under the stairs where her things were stashed, when grandmother sat up and saw her.

"How DARE you!" The abuse roared out.

With her bags slung over her shoulder, Girl ignored her, heading for the front door. She was not sneaking out like a runaway. She was going a free woman. She opened the door. Something flew through the air and caught her on the side of her head. She fell stunned. How long she lay there, she didn't know, but when her eyes flickered open Grandmother was standing over her, reaching down for her stick, which lay by Girl's side. Alarmed, head hammering pain, Girl shuffled away, back, out the door, grabbing her things as she did. The old woman reached the stick and headed towards her. How had the woman fooled them this long? She could move, she was anything but helpless.

Girl rose, staggered out across the tiles, just missing a vicious swipe of the stick. She made it to the stone steps and stepped down, down, desperation giving her strength and speed as she stepped out into the carriageway. In the distance she could see a carriage coming from town, the undertaker's hearse. Grandmother saw it too.

"THIEF! THIEF! RUNAWAY! GET THE DOGS!"

Her screams carried out over the little valley. Girl, turning to head around back to the woods where the donkey was kept, saw Grandmother shaking with fury, and realised her own world was now completely silent... In an instant, Grandmother hurled the stick.

Girl ran.

Many months later, a man called Pelletier came in from the wilderness for supplies. "There're letters for you." The storekeeper droned. Pelletier looked up from the ledger where he was checking what he owed.

"Letters?" His half brother had never written, embarrassed by his father's indiscretion. No one else would. He picked up the letters and shoved them in his pocket intending to read them later. "I'll head to the tearooms for a meal, Mac. Bundle it all together and I'll give you what I owe when I return."

Mac nodded.

Pelletier looked down as he headed out of the store; his left hand fingered the letters as if that would trace the mystery's source.

He did not see the young woman in the doorway holding a babe.

"Excuse, Madame," he muttered, the accent unmistakable. He looked up when she did not move.

She held her hand up to his face. Across the palm was tattooed a one word question,

'Pelletier?'

Part Two
Girl's Story

Outside the window, wind is blowing in pine needles. I see the swish, swish sound like my broom. I might be deaf but I can see sounds. Now my broom brushes 'cause that's what I want. I want the floor swept for my little Paulie. His hands padder, padder on the wood plank floor and he pushes himself up back, sits there looking at me just like his poor Dada. I'm not complaining. Pelletier's a good man, he's good to little Paulie. Loving, like me and Paul had, it'll take time. But it'll happen. I want it.

Here, it is very far from all the ructions over the border. I don't miss it, the fine house with its miserable occupant. I miss Paul; I grieve the tragedy of his dying in the grey, shot by his own twin, an officer in blue. I never understood that. Countrymen tearing each other apart, bloodying up their nation, their heritage. I finger Paul's bear's tooth. I wear it under my blouse, next to my heart. It's all I have of him besides our Paulie, and Paulie shall have it when grown.

Paul taught me. I still cry when I think on it. At first, I didn't understand his passion to teach me. You taught children. I was grown. I was a slave girl. Why bother? I didn't understand till I knew the depth of his love, then I realized he saw me like no other ever had - his equal. He gave me hope and I learned! Paul's lessons saved my life as much as we gave our Paulie his.

We snuck away to lessons after the house went quiet, late evening when his grandmother's snores drifted up the stairs. She hated me, my skin, my disability, but, and I'm smiling here, she had no choice did she! All the finery fretting and frittering away through her wasteful fingers. Paul's mother tutting quietly to her son but never game enough to tackle the old witch. I wish his Ma had lived. She deserved better than dying of shock – both sons gone.

Pelletier is tending his trap lines. He will be days yet. I have enough provisions and a gun. He taught me to use it. Pelletier was the illegitimate half-brother of Paul's father. A good man his 'legal' brother wanted nothing of, a bastard. Well, that's me. Unwanted daughter of a slave and a white mill manager, I'm half-caste - mulatto - a 'runaway.' A thing hunted by hounds like Pelletier's old Josh, heavy head on paws by the cooking fire… I'm glad he left Josh here. Too old to follow the lines in all weather but still strong and a good guard.

I'm writing my story in quiet moments. Why? Who'll ever see it? Maybe Paulie when he's grown. He needs to respect his roots. Paul was an educated man, Paulie will get an education too; I will teach him. Dubonnet-Maguire, for Paul's sake I kept that name by burying it in the midst of Paulie's – Paulie Dubonnet-Maguire Pelettier. He will be proud of his blood father. I will tell him, it is from Paul he got his learning and he will write his name proud!

What is my real name? Did my Ma not give me one? She died soon after having me, but I feel she must have had a name for me… must have picked a name for her girl. Her

name – I don't know. I never saw it writ. It must have been spoken around me… but my hearing was always bad. Now, talk, words, they're like annoying flies. All I get is a vague buzz of unknowing and silence. When you're just the servant, the slave girl, no one bothers. Everyone just called me 'Girl,' even my Paul.

I was passed from one poor slave family to another till I was old enough to be sold. Then the Beckers bought me. I guess they were no better nor any worse than most. Best part was being out of the fields. Then old Mr Becker started to eye me, right about the time I got my first bloods. I didn't want none of him. I knew what happened to girls silly enough to let him get his hands on them. His son sent them to auction and it was a life in the fields. I wasn't going back there. So I found a way to keep from old mister. At first I hid. It worked till my growth spurt. Then hides were scarcer. My saviour was garlic. He hated garlic. That was a revelation! A new cook, European, put it in a dish and we all thought he'd die of apoplexy! Well I'd rub it on my arms, round my neck – even rubbed it on my lips. Snuck a clove from the kitchen every night. It were my ward against the demons in that old roué.

Finally, the old man talked his son into bringing in 'new blood' and I was let go to the Dubonnet's. A mansion as had seen better times, an old harridan, Madame Ingenuie Dubonnet, her kind, beset on daughter, Jessica Maguire, and the grandson – my Paul – he liked me from the first.

I've been 'Girl' so long it is me. Pelletier asked me, when we married, if I wanted another name – he wrote in front of the priest – 'What do you want put down?' But the Church register has me as I've always been known. Girl Pelletier. I like the shape of it. I practise writing it. Paul used to say I had a 'fair' hand. He was proud of what I learned. I was too. It was my freedom, my path to here. Just not with Paul like we planned…

Those many, many months, hiding by day at first and traveling by night. The donkey Paul had hidden so carefully in the woods back of the mansion, the donkey that was to be my bearer as I got heavier with Paulie, got taken one night before I even got out of Virginia. I'd scrambled in a hollow log too tired to find a place more suited. I'd tethered the animal nearby. I sensed the men, long before the crunch of their boots and the beat of their rifle butts through the under brush vibrated round me. I froze. Runaways got no mercy. From a knothole, I peeped out and recognised the recruiter band that took Paul. I waited long hours to be sure all was clear. Then I fled on foot, wrapped in his mother's old greatcoat, with a bundle of essentials in Paul's duffle and the bear's teeth, all I had of my Paul, all there was of his twin. I travelled light; I had too far to go.

I haven't put down much about the journey in my writing. Not all the dreary, painful detail of finding food, stealing eggs, fruit, anything edible; shitting in the bushes; trying to keep a modicum of clean; the search for shelter – abandoned huts, sheds, railway carriage. Till I got too big, even scrambling in a big, old tree.

Richmond, Virginia to beyond the Great Lakes is a weary long road. The having of writing, the fact I could read saved me. Time and again, I blessed Paul for his teaching of me.

Early on, Paul taught me to read maps. He said it was a wide, wild country and one day we were going to head north, to Canada, freedom for me and the chance to be wed, impossible in the States. And we would find Pelletier, high in eastern Canada on the fringe of the Hudson Bay Company's grant.

Paul took two vital maps from his late grandfather's

collection, Phelps and Ensign's Traveller's Guide and Map of the United States and Charles DeSilver's Canada East – Lower Canada. The first, the old man acquired shortly before he died. The second, older, Paul annotated where he could. Grandfather Dubonnet's gambling addiction took him far and wide, playing fast and loose with his fortune. These maps were the most precious things he left. I hid them on me, careful and close. They were like 'Bible' for me, my guide through the unfamiliar and the wild.

The trek through the States took months, hiding from bands seeking runaways, marauders, the angry and dispossessed, seeking shelter if the weather went bad. There were close calls, like the time a band of ragged men with dangerous eyes sought shelter in the same barn as me. I felt the pound of their horse's hooves and buried myself in the hay in the loft. To my horror, two of the men found the piled up hay and made it their bed. One of them, a burly man, flung himself down across me. I muffled my cry, just in time. I lay there all night, nigh crushed by his solid weight. But he never discovered me. In moments, I felt the vibrations of his snoring. I dared not move for hours after they left, for fear they would return.

My skin, more Creole in shade, courtesy of my white father, stood by me. It made the getting of work easier. Further north there was some sympathy. Abolitionists had havens scattered across country. A few careful questions, scratched with a charcoal stub on skerricks of precious scavenged paper, found them for me.

Mid autumn, heading to northern Pennsylvania, I came to a ravaged farm. The skeleton of a woman's body lay on the porch. Had she fallen whilst fleeing marauders? Lain wounded and been finished by wolves? One arm was missing and part of a leg. Her left arm was twisted behind her where she fell back on it. I was about to step over her body when something made me stop. I pulled the arm free. Her wedding band clung to the white bones of her ring finger. I stood stock still, staring at it. I wanted it but not like most who'd sell the gold for bread. It was the taking made me hesitate. I remember, growing up on the plantations, we kids found a dead man in the woods. Old Ma saw us looking at the body and the silver fob hanging just out of his pocket. One of the boys reached for it. She waved her stick at us and yelled something as made them boys cringe. Now I reckon it for an old chant, "You dun take the Devil's due n Devil he gun come for you!" I've read about such. Anyways, whatever it were, it put the fear of God in us. We left the fob chain be.

What were more important, some superstition or what's real! I took the ring off her finger. She had no need of it now and it would stand me in good stead. Paul and I had made our vows to each other before God. But no priest had sanctioned it. Marriage were forbidden us, even in the slave-freeing North. Soon after that, he was took.

But Canada… we had hoped… I swallowed hard. This thin band would give me pass to shelter. An unwed mother was worse than a runaway. Even Abolitionists would shun her. I could feel my babe stronger now. I searched the farm for provisions – eggs, flour, mealy but edible. I corralled a nanny goat and had me some milk. A bed to sleep in, a full belly and I slept long.

I gave that place a long last look. There was too far to go yet. Too soon I'd have to shelter and wait for my little boy. The last things I took from that place – paper and pencil. Buried in back of an otherwise ransacked drawer was a small stock of a lady's letter materials.

These writing tools were my lifeline through the states. With my supply of pencils and, later, charcoal sticks, always a ready supply from any warming cooking fire, the sheets and their messages got me work, shelter, supplies. They helped me to safe paths and shorter paths. Most folk were kind. They thought me a widow of the war, which in my heart I was.

An elderly tinker, Herr Adolphus Schmidt, picked me up in his wagon near the borderlands. I had reached the end of my strength. By now any writing paper was long gone. Exhausted, I wrote a message in stones at road edge. I sat down and waited, hoping for a kind soul. It was on a lonely road, even though the main route through there. I must have fallen asleep where I sat. Next I knew, a rough, calloused hand was shaking me gently awake. He pointed at my stone words and smiled. I nodded and pointed north. He helped me into the wagon. I knew instinctively I could trust this grey, grizzled man. I slept, bumping and rocking over the rough road, grateful for every moment spared my feet and back.

I cooked. I taught him to write English, though he could read a little. They were silent lessons with letters drawn in the dirt. He was pitifully grateful. I felt the clink and clang of pots and pans behind us, their vibrations running up my arms as my fingers caressed the rickety sides of the wagon. He carried me all the way into Canada. He wrote in clumsy words and scratched pictures, how I was like his girl by an Algonquin squaw. His native wife died in childbirth and he cared for his girl, Mina, till she was taken from him. He'd gone for supplies, leaving her with friends who'd a girl a little younger. His girl had little enough chance for friendships on the road. Raiders came, took his Mina, left the rest for dead. It was on the road through Kansas. He still searched and hoped against hope to find her. Schmidt would have kept me. He made that plain – a firm warm grasp of my hands, the gentle grey-blue of his eyes. But my heart was set on Paul's plan for his child and me. I wanted a new beginning for us.

The last thing Schmidt did was take me to his wife's tribe in the Ontario and Québec borderlands. The Algonquin welcomed me. They knew of Pelletier.

Paulie was born at winter's end by the cooking fire in a birch bark wigwam. All my pent up anger, grief and loss gushed out of me on the flood of my waters and little Paulie close after.

Whilst I gathered strength and nursed my boy, I helped the family who sheltered me prepare to up their winter camp. They were heading north with the tribe after furs and to hunt. I had a request for my Algonquin host – a tattoo. He seemed amused when I drew in the embers the letters of Pelletier's name and a question mark. I pointed to my palm then to his tribal tattoos. He looked at me long with his night dark eyes. But he did what I wished.

The tattooing – stab after stab of red-hot pain took all the evening. I clenched my other hand tight, nails digging into palm and gritted my teeth. I had to be strong. This last, most dangerous part of my journey, I could not run, could not hide as easy. I had my babe and much of the country was wilderness.

The Algonquin took me with them on a spare pony over plain and pass, wildflowers now peeping through the melting ice at forest edge – a pretty time. Finally, they came within a day's journey of the white man's village, nearest to where Pelletier had last been seen by their local kin. For Schmidt's sake, I think, they gave me the pony. Not a small gift from these stern people.

Paulie in an Indian papoose, I rode the rough wagon track into the town. Shadow fingers were stealing the day by the time I enquired at the general store – writing my enquiry on some newsprint. Whilst the scrawny weathered storekeeper read my message and pondered, I read the headlines in the old paper. The war had ended. The Confederacy had lost. They said that meant freedom for folks the likes of me. Did that mean my Paul died for naught. Tears welled. I shook my head, set my jaw and looked up. Little Paulie's father, my Paul, gave us our chance for freedom. That's what mattered. I would fight anything to keep it.

After what seemed an age, the storekeeper started to speak. Stopped, not realizing I had some lip reading, and started to write. Pelletier had called in briefly some weeks ago for supplies. He had headed north.

Schmidt had given me some coins and a few notes he could ill afford but had insisted. I used these now to get some foodstuffs and a Bowie knife, nodded at the storekeeper and left. I leaned my map of Canada's East on the flank of my pony and tried to figure where Pelletier might have headed. I decided to keep north and check again at the next town. With some weeks gone, maybe he would call for supplies and the next town was bigger. I knew Paul had written to his uncle, telling of his plans and of me, not long before recruiters took him. Had Pelletier ever received it?

The ride north was quiet. I had had years of seeking my own company in preference to that of others. The deaf and to all purposes mute, are not understood by most. There is no patience with us. That was till Paul and his mother. They had shown me something different. I had responded like a flower opening to the sun. It changed me. Now I was in strange territory and with my baby. I felt alone in a new way. Care of another can open you, vulnerable, exposed. Even so, if harm came, I would fight for my son until I could not move.

I could see the town in the distance, when I became aware of someone following me. The vibrations rose through the ground. The wind, which was blowing from the south, carried scent – dirty, unwashed man-scent. I spurred the pony on. The vibrations became stronger, the scent more concentrated. I glanced over my shoulder and looked into eyes flint hard not a length behind me. What those eyes said was nightmare.

I felt for the knife, gripped and drew it out. Clutched it to me. I would not reveal it yet, not unless he came up beside of me, unless he acted. I wouldn't risk him drawing a gun.

Long, hammering moments he drew by. I saw his arm reach out for the reigns and struck, slashing open his arm - blood spurted furious and hot. His mouth shaped a scream with the unexpectedness of my strike and drew back in a snarl. I glanced over, saw him reach his other hand for his gun. I wove the horse, praying he could not aim as well with his left. Then, from the town, a cloud of dust advancing, he saw it too and veered off.

The group of hunter-traders drew level. We reigned. Too breathless with fright, it was all I could do to hold my hand up in greeting and query. Their leader saw, nodded, pointed. Pelletier was in town. They saw the blood on my knife, reigned their animals back, drew their guns and they rode down the way I'd come. There was a volley of shots. Any man as would harm mother and child met with frontier justice!

I rode my pony hard. I would not risk Pelletier leaving before me, not again. I pulled into the town and headed for the general store. Moments later, I tied the pony at the rail out front and almost ran up the wood steps just as a tall man with grey flecking his beard emerged. He begged pardon as he sought to pass. I held my palm up, right in his face. He stopped, amazed, looked hard at me, a slow smile curling the corner of his mouth. He nodded and said one word, "Pelletier!" I never saw a word form on lips so welcome before. I reached out, unable to stop myself, and touched those lips. I was home…

Part Three
The Making of Me

Ma went first. They dragged her into the barn and we didn't see it but we heard every scream, every thud, then when they'd had enough, the shot, the silence.

Pa heard it all, looked away from me and Jem, gleaming streaks of tears cutting a path through the dirt on his leathery face.

I don't want to tell of Pa's end.

I saw it all. Jem made not a sound. I wondered if he'd gone blind or something. Reckon I cried it all for us. Screaming, begging was no use, there were no mercy in any of 'em and, if we lived, I'd have to fend for Jem too.

They didn't kill Jem and me. One yelled over his shoulder as they rode out, "An you see, we'll be back! We'll sell y's!" They all laughed loud and dirty like. They left us, house ransacked, barn burning, animals slaughtered or taken off with them. We stood in the yard for, dunno, could have been hours after they went. Pa's blood'd seeped in the soil and was just a dark stain. I wanted to bury him but I was ten and it were just too hard.

Dark reached out and took hold of everything. Chill

set in. Jem pulled at my jacket. I ignored him. I didn't want to move. Moving meant I acknowledged everything'd changed, meant moving on and I didn't want to. I wanted it all to go back, back to before the Raiders came.

Jem didn't let up. He pulled and kept pulling. Then he did something I almost hit him for. He yelled. Yelled with all the power in his three year old lungs.

"Shut up! Shut Up!" I hissed the words at him, in his face. "You want they come back? You want to be dead?"

"HUNGWY!" He shouted it at me, his cherubic lips all pouty in a way Ma could never resist.

I just stared at him. Full moon lit up his stubborn little face. No sign of a tear or a torment.

Hadn't he seen anythin', and the noise of death....

"Hungwy!"

Then I remembered somethin' Gramps'd said to us before he died. He was abed and just a shrunken bag o' bones, but his eyes, still fierce blue and his hand steady.

He'd asked for his old letters he and Grandma'd writ each other whilst he was off fighting the Indian Wars. They were in his trunk under the bed. I'd found them and, cause I was curious, went to pull out his old blue coat. His medals fell out. He never wore 'em. He kept 'em hid, never talked about the wars.

I asked him about the medals.

All he said was, "I pray for forgiveness and the Memory Taker to do his blessed work." Pa said the farm was Gramps' haven from the horrors as he called 'em.

At Gramps' burial, I asked Father Xavier what he meant by the Memory Taker. Was he a saint? Father smiled down from his spindly height, "Why, ma boy, I think as it'll be St Thomas of Villanova, poor man had a terrible memory and I think, I think, he just might lose memories we don't want. I

think your poor Gramps had more 'n a few of them!"

Maybe the Memory Taker'd looked after Jem.

I knew there'd be no food in the house. The Raiders'd taken all.

Stepping around poor Pa's body, quiet and reverent like, I took Jem to the house. I made him use the commode and found us warm stuff. We'd need it. We had to leave. They just might come back.

On the floor, I found a crust of stale bread they'd dropped in their hurry. I gave that to Jem. It shut him up. I filled a bottle with water from the pump over the trough. We left.

I took him out to the main road that passed our place, many miles from the nearest town, south of us, Lawrence. It was dark but full moon lit for us. I kept to the shadows.

We'd walked till I had to carry Jem. Only fear kept me struggling step on step.

I heard a noise, odd, a furious muffled clopping down the wagon ruts. I looked back. Even in that light I could make out Adolphus Schmidt's caravan. The horse had cloth bound over its hooves, the muffled sound. It were the tinker, we all knew, the tinker and his motherless girl. She was older'n me but short, tawny skinned, cheerful. Ma reckoned she were married Mina's age. But Mina played with me all the same, dangled Jem on her knee or pig-a-backed him horse rides.

I stepped out in the road quick and waved and called "Herr Schmidt! Herr Schmidt!"

He seen us. He slowed to a walk and drew up. "Vas is? Where your Mama, Papa? Undt Jem? 'Es too liddle to be oot here!"

"Dead"

"Vass you sayin'?"

"Dead, Raiders!"

"Mein Gott! Get in! Kvick! Kvick!" He jumped down and bundled us both in helter skelter, pulling a slice of dry rye bread from his bread bin. Jem was stirring. He pushed it into Jem's fat little hand and Jem started sucking at it, still half asleep.

"Ve go! Kvick! Kvick!"

"Where's Mina?"

"M'be dead, dunno."

"Where…"

He cut me off, his voice breaking, "Don' you ask, liddle vun."

He said nothing more but drove that horse fast as its sturdy legs would go over the bumps and ridges.

Jem fell back to sleep of a mercy. I sat up and stared into the night. I had visions of poor Mina lying like Pa. I felt the tears wash down my face but nothing would wash away those memories. Some things hid like a jag of glass in your stomach. Nothing'd loose it and the pain never went.

I slept fitfully till near dawn. We'd come to a burnt out farm. Herr Schmidt took his caravan rattling through the gate and into the shell of a barn.

"Why we here?"

"Them Raiders been. There's nothin' for 'em left. We be here till nightfall. Liddle Jem, he sleep?"

"Yeah."

"You helps me then. Fill water bottles at the pump. I set snare."

Herr Schmidt was good at hunting with snares and traps and his knife. He never had a gun. He taught me to set snares. He got us a two brace of quail for eating. Cooked it in the ground, no smoke to speak of and the smoldering in part of the barn hid that.

I swear Jem out ate me. I had to pull the meat from

the little bones so he didn't choke his silly self, he gobbled so fast.

"MORE!"

"Shhh!" I picked at the bones and he grabbed as fast, I swear, as he'd never eaten and stuffed it in with his fat, greasy little fingers, plastering his face with the warm juiciness of the meat. He ate till his eyes drooped and he sank back to sleep. I guess all the stuff as happened plain tuckered him out.

Herr Schmidt gave me a wet rag to polish his little face and fingers. Herr Schmidt liked things, "All ship shape 'n shiny, dat's it! Juz like the pots 'n pans!"

His pans were all wrapped, noiseless now in blankets and sheets, not like when we knew him and Mina. Once or twice a year he'd come, banging and jangling happy tin music off of the sides of his van. We'd loved his visits. Ma always got a pan or pot, spoon or ladle, even if she didn't really need it. It was so grand havin' visitors with news and we'd have a slap up meal and Mina'd play with us like she were our big sis, 'cept, I were near tall as Mina…

"How long afore we's safe?"

"We's a way a bit ta go boy. Outa Kansas not so far, but we go nights, not so fast."

Jem was a 'pack o monkeys' what Herr Schmidt reckoned. Keeping him quiet, outa trouble was no fun. I was glad t' see the sun go hiding behind the jagged tooth top of the barn. We finished what was left of those quails and buried the bones. Water bottles full, some eggs found'n cooked in the ground and some old carrots I found in the wreck of the kitchen garden. We were all in the caravan and Herr Schmidt's horse hitched up when he froze. His face white like a snow sky. I opened my mouth, but he put his hand on my lips. Then I heard it. Distant like thunder in the hills, rolling… and…

voices…

I looked across at Jem. He was lying quiet, tummy full and tuckered out. I followed Herr Schmidt's eyes out to the hills where the noise was gathering, spreading, rising in dust clouds. Men on horseback!

"Childens, we movin' now!"

"Where?"

"Nort, nort to union, outa Kansas." Herr Schmidt hugged his boys, as he called Jem 'n me, "We don' want no more bloods."

With dark barely on us and that rumbling and rattling of hooves and clattering of metal, enough to put the fear of everythin' into you, we snuck out. But the noise came no closer. They weren't comin' our way. Of a mercy, they were comin' from the east and headed down a ways to Lawrence about the night's ride away.

Herr Schmidt reckoned they were a raiding party heading to join up to something bigger. There'd been rumours of Raider vengeance on Lawrence for its abolitionist stand and other stuff. "Didn't matter," Herr Schmidt said, "Warrin' men'll al'ys have a reason t' fight."

We traveled all night with just the clop, clop of the horse and the odd spooky call of an owl off somewhere in the dark. The yowl of coyote and the howl of the wolves seemed to follow us. They always made the little hairs on back of my neck go prickle. Gramps used ta tell some awful scary stories about the wolves… he reckoned his Pa told him how, one hard winter in the War of Independence, the wolves ate the bodies of the dead laying in the field afore their blood could freeze. I kept lookin' over at Herr Schmidt and was I ever glad he was there, every stolid, stocky bit on 'im set there just drive, drive drivin' that old horse to save us.

One other thing happened. I don't want to tell of it but

I'm gonna. Father Xavier said sometimes, when you can, to talk is to throw the bad out so it don't hang like a big, stinkin' bird round your neck. Didn't know what he meant by that till I read this poem 'bout a seaman and an albatross later at school.

We were clopping along, but more hushed like 'cause Herr Schmidt wrapped scraps of blanket round his horse's hooves. It were so quiet you'd hear wings beat and sound like a far storm comin'. Off of the side of the road, we heard somethin'.

What's that?" I hissed.

"We not worry, Shhh!"

"Sounds like something hurt..." The noise was a moaning sort of cry.

"Not our worry."

"Father Xavier says you gotta help folks what's in need of it. You helped me 'n Jem. We gotta help. Supposin' it were Mina?"

Herr Schmidt pulled the reigns hard. The horse stopped with a jolt that rolled Jem round the back of the wagon. Miracle of miracles, he didn't stir!

"You stay here. I go. "

I saw him unsheath his knife and he climbed down.

"I not back you count 400. You take wagon, you go."

I think the cold of night, the sounds that sneak in your ear and stick in your brain like hissing ghosts made me count quicker. Thing was I got to 400 and no Herr Schmidt. I couldn't go, not and leave that kind man, who saved Jem 'n me.

I drove the horse and cart, careful like, off the side of the road round under a big, old tree. I hoped it wasn't too obvious there.

Down I got and went where the noise'd come from. In

a bit of a clearing, there was Herr Schmidt all leant over a man. He wasn't in uniform. As I got closer, I recognized one of our far neighbours, 'Leanman' Jack as Pa called him. Herr Schmidt heard me and leapt up, knife ready.

"Ah yer fool kid! I coulda stabbed yer! What ya doin' here?"

"I got to 400…"

Herr Schmidt 'd forgot all about me countin'.

"Oi, vell I'm glad y's came then." He smiled and I saw he'd been crying.

" Mr Lehman, 'e says, Mina ain't dead…"

I stared at him. I didn't understand.

"Sometimes is better dead."

I went over to Mr. Lehman and knelt beside him.

"What's he sayin', Leanman Jack?"

"She were took. His Mina's took." Leanman's voice cracked but he kept on, "She and the Wimmer girl were pickin' wildflowers in the back field neighbouring our place. They grabbed 'em. My wife 'n kids were off visiting, thanks God." Leaman paused to catch his breath and grimaced. "Me myself, I weren't fightin' all o' them. I ran for help. One on 'em shot me. I laid like dead. The men had other things on their minds. They didn't bother more with me. I blacked out. When I come to, they were gone. I dragged meself here. Dunno what happened to the Wimmers and their girl. Jus' afore I passed out, I saw one on 'em ride off wi' Mina"

Leanman Jack started coughing something chronic then and groaned awful as graveyards.

"They got my Mina. They be gonna sell her for sure, if she still..."

Mina's Ma was Indian so her skin was sorta dark. I knew what 'sell her' meant. Pa'd told me of the slave auctions. We used to have an old dark man work for us till he died. Ma said Pa bought him of a pity. Pity or no, old Ben did his best for us and he was like family. Pa'd tell him now and then he could go, he was free. All Ben'd say was, "Where I go? No family here. You all I got." And he was 'family' till we laid 'im to rest next to little Jane, my sister as died a baby.

"What we doin'?" I crinkled my face, all serious.

"We get Mr Lehman to a doctor or he's gonna lose 'e's leg!"

"What we doin' 'bout Mina?"

Herr Schmidt rounded on me, he almost screamed, "Vat you t'ink I do!" He sank to his knees, "Can do nuthink…."

I looked helplessly at Leanman Jack. He's gotten his self up on one arm and was holdin' his side. He sort of gasped out between breaths, "'E's right boy. All we c'n do's tell first Unioners we see, then tell whoever'll hear. They'll sell her south, way south for sure."

"Pray?" I sez my voice all broken like.

"Yes, boy, lot o that." Leanman Jack collapsed back and no one said anything.

Me and Herr Schmidt kind of half dragged, half carried Leanman Jack to where I'd hid the wagon and got him in with a lotta cries and cusses and me prayin' no Raiders was about.

Herr Schmidt did what he could for Leanman Jack but the leg was awful! All smashed with the ball and bits of bone and gore and flesh. Jem woke as Herr Schmidt was tryin' to clean the wound and dig out the ball. I never seen a man vomit with pain till then.

Jem took one look at Leanman Jack and screamed! Poor man were groanin' like to wake the dead and Jem right in 'is ear like to keep the rest of humankind awake! I did my best.

"Ve's best goin'…" Herr Schmidt looked at me like I was his right-hand man.

I felt in me self like I grew right then – you measured

me, I reckon an inch!

"It's good, Herr Schmidt, I'll look after Leanman Jack 'n Jem."

He smiled, patted me on the shoulder, climbed up front and we jolted off again.

The steady jolt, jolt of the wagon over ruts and bumps shut up Jem better'n I could, though I did think of Herr Schmidt's schnapps bottle. Sometimes, I caught him having a swig. He'd see me and say "For the pain, boy." And I knew it was that inside pain, the glass jag pain deep in and I thought, maybe the Memory Taker used schnapps, but Herr Schmidt'd never given me a drop tho' I asked.

Down the road a ways, the schnapps did come out.

Not two days bare gone, Leanman Jack was groanin' weaker and sweat and a palour, all mask like, on 'im.

Herr Schmidt looked at the wound and shook his head, "Nicht gut…" shakin' his head the while. The smell from the wound were real bad and the colour of the lower leg enough to puke.

"Doctor? We used ter have a Dr. Cronkite …"

"He joined the Union," whispered Mr. Lehman, "Heard he were dead."

I looked at Herr Schmidt. He took a deep breath, squared his shoulders and looked hard at Leanman Jack. "We gotta do it."

The two men held each other's gaze like things 'd been said afore when I wasn't in hearin'.

"Off…?" was all poor Mr Lehman said.

"Yar…" Herr Schmidt turned and put both his hands firm on my shoulders.

"I got to give your Jem a goot sleepin'. I give 'im schnapps."

My eyes near popped. He hadn't given me a drop!

"Yer see, weez gotta take dat leg orf!'

I looked from Herr Schmidt to Leanman Jack and back. You juz don't take a leg off.

"Gangrene..." Mr. Lehman's voice was weak. "It'll kill me if 'n we don't. Adolphus and I talked on it last night."

"How much... off?" my voice sounded like this sissy squeak.

The ball'd gone in below the knee but the colour and the smell... Leanman Jack called it 'gas gangrene'.

Herr Schmidt made camp deep in the woods and set a pot on to boil. He put his knife blade, the axe and a saw he had in the boiling water. Mr. Lehman didn't look. He just asked, sort of pleading, 'Sharp, good 'n sharp?"

"Yar, sharp..." Herr Schmidt nodded and patted my shoulder. I think he was trying to put some of his own strength into me. I knew why soon enough.

Herr Schmidt made poor Leanman Jack comfortable as he could. He put schnapps with a pile of sugar and milk we'd gotten from a stray cow the Raiders missed. He gave it to Jem patient, like my Ma would've. Jem looked up at him and smiled this angel's smile and fell back, out to it.

Herr Schmidt kissed 'is little forehead and turned to me. "Com'n."

With his arm round my shoulder, he led me to the fire and proceeded to lay the knife, axe and saw out on a clean sheet.

He gave poor Leanman Jack the rest of the schnapps, loving like he was a ministerin' angel.

Herr Schmidt led me round back and said, "All yer body weight, on is arms. Yer've to ter keep 'im vrom movin'."

I said nothing but tears at the horror of it were streaming down my cheeks. It had to be done. Deep down I knew, no choice.

I took a deep breath, prayed and wished I'd gotten some of them schnapps.

Herr Schmidt studied the leg a moment. Made 'is decision, 'e was goin' for speed. He said to me later he reckoned it were kinder.

He signalled me to get Leanman Jack's attention, picked up the axe, squared himself and struck!

Lehman screamed, jolted up and fell back, out cold.

It was severed just above the knee. Blood spurted all over!

Grabbing a smooth, strong piece of wood he'd had in the fire, Herr Schmitt plunged it in the wound. The blood oozed a mere trickle. Poor Leanman Jack's body shuddered but he were still out cold.

Herr Schmidt used the saw and knife to trim the ragged bits off the wound and bandaged it up tight, real, real tight. Then, quietly, as if he were polishing pans, he cleaned the axe, the saw, the knife and buried the leg.

While Leanman Jack was out, he got me to help him lug Leanman's limp body up into the wagon.

I laid myself down beside Mr Lehman and held his hand. Don't know why. It just seemed right.

He didn't come round till light was seeping over the far hills. Herr Schmidt said he was going to try and find folks to care for poor Leanman Jack. We were coming north near the border of Kansas, crossing the corner of Missouri into Iowa.

Iowa was a haven compared to where we'd been. We left Mr Lehman in a military hospital in Keokuk. The army surgeon were so impressed, he asked Herr Schmidt to stay on and help. I don't know what happened to Leanman Jack, but I hope he lived and saw his family again.

Herr Schmidt took Jem 'n me north and left us with

Lutheran friends of his in Dubuque, Iowa. Then he headed across into Illinois. He told me he hoped this strong Union state might help him find his Mina.

"Even she dead, I brings her home…" I miss him and I miss Mina. I'll never see Ma an' Pa no more. I hope I sees Herr Schmidt an' his girl.

The Weisse were kind folk. They managed to write to my Ma's cousin in Pennsylvania. She wrote back months later, she didn't want us, she had twelve kids on her own. Her husband been taken, courtesy the war.

Those Lutheran folk kept us and fed us and I worked in their shop. Jem never did remember aught of the Raiders and the day we lost Ma and Pa. He asks for them less and less, till now it's not much. I talked to Herr Weisse once about it. I told him of St Thomas, the Memory Taker. He said he thought he must be a busy saint in this godforsaken time.

Sometimes, I wonder if I'll ever go back to our farm and bury Ma and Pa. I think of Mina. Herr Schmidt traveled the Southern states looking for her. He ain't found her, yet… He went back to Kansas just once but no one knowed what happened to Mina. Sometimes he goes north, Canada. It's where his wife were from. She were Algonquin and he reckoned they were 'family'. Maybe, if she got away, Mina'd head there. When I'm growed, maybe I'll go with him an' look for Mina.

There's times I wonder why the Memory Taker don't work for me. At first, there were nights I'd wake screaming and wet, Frau Weisse'd comes in and her big cushion arms'd muffle up my crying. I know she meant well, but then I'd just wanna scream it out! I don't wake screamin' no more. Pa reckoned I was a sickly babe, come too early. He made me help, even tho' Ma said I weren't strong enough. I got strong in the arms but it's not the same as strong in the head. Life is what makes you strong that way. Sometimes, I think that journey through Kansas was the making of me. No one will ever call me weak. I seen too much.

Part Four
Mina

Pounding, pounding, pounding hooves off in the distance and coming nearer, never bothered me once. I love horses. Papa says I have a gift with them. I can tell how they're being ridden and somewhat of the rider from the beat of the hooves. These horses were being driven hard. Closer, and the cussing of men sounded above the echo of hooves. It seemed to be coming around us two sides through the woods. Raiders! Lisa and I grabbed each other and fled through the field, back towards the safety of the barn. We thought.

An arm grabbed me up and threw me across a saddle that stank of man sweat and blood. I could see Lisa swooped up the same as she were no more'n a sack of chaff and a thin one at that. The man as took her, leered at me. A flap of lank, black hair flopped across his face, momentarily hiding a sabre slash on his cheekbone.

The horses thundered across the field. Someone fired a shot, yelling, "Got 'im!" We pulled up sharp in the farmyard, dust flying up in clouds, obscuring the farmhouse door from our view a long moment. The dust settled. Silence. Lisa's parents, the Wimmers stood in the doorway, clutching each other, staring at their daughter and the dirty, blood-spattered men.

Two shots and the Wimmers fell. The men dismounted. One grabbed Lisa. "Come on, Dicky Boy!"

The man who had me over his saddle steadied his horse. "This here's too young. You take the pretty one." Lisa was dragged crying and screaming into the barn. The man who'd grabbed me turned his horse and took off for the fields.

Someone yelled behind him. Another, "Let him go, we got the good 'un!"

I had heard the adults talk about what happened if brigands got you. "Lisa! You... You can't leave her!" I strained to see into his face.

"She's good as dead. You want to live? Shut up, lie still."

The man said nothing more. Once in the woods, he cut up a rug and wrapped the horses hooves. He slowed the horse, as darkness crept up on us. "We head for the River. You want to live, you my daughter. Understand." I looked down at my tawny arms, a shade off my Algonquin mother, about the colour of his.

Papa and I were down Kansas, trying to get further north, away from the fury of the war. Papa left me with the Wimmers, whilst he went for supplies. We were north of Lawrence, not far from where the Kansas and Missouri rivers met. Papa, poor Papa, he'd think me dead. The thought of what he would see on his return, made me dry retch, brown, bitter fluid down the horse's mane. My captor didn't flinch.

"We go north."

"You, a Confederate! Why..."

His hand wrapped over my mouth. His thin hooked nose squashed into my face, his black eyes flashing, as he hissed, "You not talk sides. No side. We side whoever's loudest guns.

Understand?"

I brushed off his hand. Realisation dawned, "You're circus!" Gypsies and circus folk knew no 'side' in this war, a good survival tactic for travelers. "Why you with the Raiders?"

"I ain't! I stole shirt and kepi off a man needed it no more. They seen me in the woods, thought me deserter. Told 'em as I's a scout got cut off from me company!" He had to stop himself laughing, his voice still no more'n a harsh whisper, "Smart li'l git, ain't ya!" He flicked out his knife, a beauty. He saw my admiring glance.

"Knife thrower." I looked up and smiled, my relief genuine. Papa and I knew most of the troupes that worked the states thereabouts. We camped with them, shared stories and I minded their young-uns, even helped a birth when the midwife were drunk. Papa once told me, I'd an old head for my age. I was then fourteen years. I'm sixteen now, though stockiness belies my age.

I talked circus, asked after folk, all the while looking that rough-neck straight in the eyes. Pepi, as I found out his name to be, knew most of them.

"Yeah… You not afraid o' Pepi are yer! We're headed for Delavan." Accepted, simple as that! This were a safer way, me and Pepi.

I'd heard of the winter home for circuses, Great Lakes side of Wisconsin. I wondered if he might leave me at Dubuque. It sat right squat at the edge of three states and had a large German community. Papa had friends there, good friends.

The river, still swollen, dirty from rain and downwash had burst its banks. I looked at Pepi. He were chewing the inside of his cheek like he were thinking. Papa used to do that, especially if we had no chicory root. We roasted that for coffee but Papa used to keep back some, lighter roasted, to chew on.

Pepi stiffened. Then I heard it, hooves, distant, coming our way steady like. I felt Pepi's body tense. He gripped the back of my neck, told me to look out the river.

THWACK!

A sickening thud and next I knew I was across the front of the saddle part cradled in his right arm and my head fit to split. I moaned loud.

"What's the matter with 'er?"

The smell of horses and man sweat strong in my nostrils, I barely opened my eyes but enough to see soldiers, Confederates.

"My daughter, her horse spook, she fall, bang her head bad. You see!"

One of the men pushed my head. He let go when I cried out.

"Mmm, it weren't for ya gal, we'd have the horse. Get going."

Pepi dug his heels in, the horse jumped forward and took off.

At the river, we made it to a landing still intact, and waited off in the brush. Pepi roughly washed and bandaged my head. I said nothing. I'd gathered enough to know my bloodied bandage gave us passage.

The steamer pulled in full of soldiers and stores and camp followers. Pepi and I shuffled in among wounded being ferried out and supplies, headed to wherever folk fought or fled. This was no floating hotel of the bold and garish kind I'd heard about from travelers' fireside stories. It's one time grandeur was gone, paint chipped, gilt edgings all but worn away like the vestiges of an old tart's former looks. Now, it was a working boat, a goods ferry that ran the blockades by night with lights out and the men aboard as dark and desperate as the times required.

Pepi kept a firm grip on my arm, the other on the horse's reins. Those menfolk eyed us in ways that meant no good. I thought of Lisa and clenched my teeth. I wasn't about to cry here. Maybe we oughtn't have kept the horse… it made us so conspicuous.

My head still throbbed. Pepi curled me down amidst a pile of tarpaulins on the deck and threw a horse-blanket over me. "You sleep now. You good girl. No time later. We move, we like wind on water."

Hours later, I felt something warm, sticky, drop, drop, drop on my face. I blinked through sleep-heavy eyes. Moonlight showed Pepi leaned over against me, his prickly cheek grazing my forehead, the blood running from a great ,crooked gash in his throat. The horse - gone.

Off to one side, I could hear low, rough talk. As my head cleared, I realized the talk was about me.

"The gypsy's dead. Sell his girl ta traders, she'll fetch a good sum."

"Not till I have 'er first."

"She's too young for that."

"Where I's from they's married aready hern age."

I had no idea how far to the next landing, nor how many we'd already passed. No idea how far down river we were, or if we'd made the turn to the big river. The surety was, if I stayed here, I were to be sold to slavers. I ferreted round mouse quiet. Here, I found Pepi's knife, still in its sheath. He must've been jumped whilst sleeping. I stuck it down my front.

Most owners of the voices plotting my future, had their

backs turned from me. I raised myself gently and glanced over the side. Shore was a swim away, but a swim back to where I'd come aboard. There were no help for it. I readied myself, jumped and swam for all I was worth against the drag under towards the paddlewheel.

I doubt they heard me over the splash of the blades, or, if they did, they didn't mark it. Shore loomed only strokes away when I heard the cry go up from the steamer, "Overboard!"

Dragging myself ashore under overhang, I hoped I couldn't be seen from the boat. The water hugged my clothes, cold and dripping about me like furls of dying flowers. Off a ways, I could see the glow of a small fire among trees. I decided I'd head there. At worst, I could steal something useful, at best there might be help. I were not that sure the men might not come after me.

An old Quaker couple huddled over the little fire, stirring something that smelled of meat and herb. Off behind them, part hidden in the trees, were a solid farm horse, the sort that pulled ploughs, and a covered wagon.

I deliberately stood on twigs, so the noise alerted them of my coming. The old man looked up, his hand instinctively going for a large stick at his feet. He saw me and reached across to his wife instead.

"Martha!" low and urgent.

She looked up, and then in the direction he pointed.

"Oh, child, come here!"

"Shush woman, thou knowest not who else is maybe here."

"It's just me." I walked up to the fire and invited myself to sit down, warming my hands without so much as 'by your leave'. 'Never give folks a chance to say, naye.' It were a byword among tinkers, like Papa.

That were the whole of how I became the 'niece' of

Martha and Jed. They were heading back to their community, the opposite direction to where I hoped my father might be - if he still lived. They had headed east to visit relatives in the Carolinas and the war trapped them on their return to the southwest, Indiana.

We got on well enough. I made myself useful without asking. We travelled nights, mostly, and kept from the roads by day. The tear and gash of war was everywhere, charcoal and ashes and brokenness.

We had journeyed some days and rounded a hill. Up on the horizon, a tree, or, more correct, a shell of what it was before lightning or cannon struck, bore a strange, unnatural decoration. A body, swayed in the wind, the great limb creaking with the burden of the dead weight. We looked up at it, Jed and me. Martha crossed herself and would go nowhere near the body 'cept to beg Jed cut it down for Christian burial.

The face was burnished with drying in the sun, bar a bright scar on the cheekbone. Crows had eaten out the eyes, but I recognized the man as took Lisa, and felt not a wisp of sorrow for his soul.

I told Jed in a hushed voice as we dug the grave. He glanced over his shoulder to where Martha stood apart, praying softly. "Don't thee be telling her now, she's enough sorrow on her old heart. We buried all our own. Our eldest child last summer – a stray bullet they said. But I doubt it were."

When it were done, and it took a whiles with Martha's prayers and tears for the departed, Jed hung the man's army tag about the upright of the rough wood cross and they left. I hung back a moment, enough to grab that cursed tag and hurl it high and wide away. It caught high up in a tree down slope.

No varmint like that deserved any sort of memorial.

Crows circled the site, their tattered wings like blackened fragments from infernal fires. We could still hear them over the next rise, loudly objecting to the loss of their carrion feast.

During the lull in our journey, I thought long and hard about where I were headed and what I would do. It were fool's work to journey back aways now. Finding Papa, if he still lived, would have to wait till war's end, if it ever came.

Jed and Martha treated me well. They wanted me to come with them to Indiana, as family but I hoped I still had my Papa. I decided, with their help, I would find employment and wait out the war in northwestern Kentucky, then seek Papa, unless he found me first! Did it not work out, I would head to Indiana and a welcome.

Autumn was some kind of reprieve from major battles in Kentucky and nobody minded an old Quaker couple and their young charge clopping into town with their raggedy wagon and big boney old farm horse.

We called at the local store and barely got in the door when the owner, a spider of a man with arms and legs that reached to where's most needed ladders, strode into our path, barring our way.

"It'll do yer no good. Confederate's took most o' the lot and what was left the Union's got."

"Our needs are small, sir, some beans, flour, chicory." The owner opened his mouth to protest but Jed started up again, proud and straight, "We can pay!"

"And I'm looking for work." I tilted my head back to see up into his face, all beak like nose and bright small eyes. I barely reached the man's ribcage.

"Work! You, young miss. Well be glad yer not got pants or you'd be in kepi 'n boots, if you could find any!" He seemed to think this funny. His laughter rang around the high ceilings and bounced along the rafters.

Someone coughed politely. We all turned to look in the direction. A portly, well dressed man with walrus moustache and a leather bag gripped in his other hand, tipped his hat to Martha and introduced himself, "Dr. Stanislof Wilkolski, at your service. Ma'am, Sir, I believe, I might have work for your young lady. I am heading out to Mandolin, the Maguire ranch. Young Mrs Maguire is about to birth and I expect it to go hard with her. Not …" he paused, "built for it. They'll be in need of a strong young lass to help with the babe."

I had helped with the little ones when Papa and I visited Mother's tribe. I'd been at births. Babies were the same world over. Feed 'em. Wind 'em. Wipe 'em and rock 'em to sleep.

"I can do that!" I smiled at Martha and Jed.

The doctor coughed, "We need to leave now. That alcohol…"

The store owner's hands went to his hips and his sloping forehead creased in so many folds his hairline near met his eyebrows, "Now Dr…"

"I know you have it, Bronski!"

With a grimace, Bronski ambled round behind the counter and drew out a dusty bottle from some hidden crevice.

"And whilst you're about it, these good folk need little."

Jed and Martha thanked him and hugged me. I left them as I found them, with only Pepi's knife, still in its sheath, but now tucked securely in my belt. As we left the store, Martha hurried after and grabbed my arm. She pressed on me her Sunday best, for meeting coat, as a parting gift. Her only luxury, I knew this was more than just a thoughtful gift. It were acknowledging me as more, it said I were family. I hugged her the tighter and ran after Dr. Wilkowski, jumping up beside him on his gig as he flicked whip, shook reins and off.

I remembered the Kentucky hills, the green and loveliness, from the days with Papa, trundling the rough roads in our wagon, the pots and pans jangling their welcoming song around us. Now autumn dragged its last bright leaves through wisps of winter chill. I hugged that coat around me like it were Martha herself. Though I had no wish to admit it yet, I felt deep down it was our parting. The future reached out to me, drawing me down the road to Mandolin.

We were on the approach road, when a rider flashed down from the distant ranch, legs flailing and hand whipping the horse's flanks. He started yelling, well before we made out a word of it. The good doctor's face set stern and he hurried the horse much as he dared in the war-pitted track.

As the rider drew up, we caught his words, "She's bad. Real bad! Maguire's like a man possessed…"

"Get back! Tell him we're here. Get sheets, boiling water…"

And the man was gone, belting back the way he came and yelling as loud, though none would hear him for a mile yet. The good doctor coughed, "You're a sensible girl. This is not a regular situation. Maguire's a widower and the young lady you're about to meet is a…" he paused, glanced at me sidelong, then continued, having made up his mind, I guessed, that I kept a sober tongue in my head. He gave another cough, "well, just call her an adventuress. Maguire hoped to steady her and marry, but…"

"It's alright, doctor, I understand." He looked genuinely relieved. My travels with my father took us into frontier territory and I knew exactly what an 'adventuress' might be!

The journey continued in silence.

My hands dug deep into the pockets of Martha's coat, whether for warmth or to draw on some inner resource, I know not. My fingers closed round something, a comb! Instinctively, I pulled it out, finding it to be handsome, inlaid with pearl shell. I swept my hair up and fastened it tight. The doctor must have glimpsed my action and gave a nod. "Makes you out older, lass. For now, that is good."

Tall trees lined the lead road into the homestead. I reckoned twenty years growth, their shadows striping the carriageway in a fretwork that reminded me of old country lace. Good-looking horses grazed the grasslands either side. I wondered to myself how Maguire had kept them from the military. More than that, I had no time, the sweep of homestead with its wide, white verandahs and tall gables swung into view.

An agitated serving man met us and led us up the sweep of steps to the ornately columned portico. Through the open door came sobs and screams… We followed the sounds up the stairs, we did not have to be shown the way.

Maguire, or so I supposed from the stature and command of the man, gripped the doctor's lapels, "What kept you so long!"

"Now, now man, steady yourself!" Dr. Wilkowski brushed Maguire aside, "You know the roads. A horseman at speed risks much, for a gig it's pure folly."

Setting himself on the bed beside the pale young woman, he pulled his stethoscope out of his bag and listened to her stomach. He nodded and proceeded to examine her. The eyes of her I'll not forget, wild, like some forest creature trapped.

She'd gone quiet, when we arrived, but now she started to screaming and the filth that flowed out was fit for camp followers and rowdies.

Maguire seemed embarrassed, till he saw we paid no mind. I was already busying myself with basins of hot water and more heating, sheets and strips for binding. The doctor, apronned now, was setting instruments ready… in case.

Hours later, things were no better and the young woman had sunk into a feverish sleep. Maguire's manservant, McGinty, brought us a light supper of bread and potato with thick bean soup and real coffee fortified with what, from the smell, I suspected were whiskey. I made sure I ate first afore I downed that.

During this time, I took in my surrounds, the man of the house and the young woman. Everything was well appointed, quality but not lavish, though I suspected from his taste and not hers. The jewelry on her fingers and the charms about her neck were of a rich but gaudy make. She looked like a porcelain doll that had been over painted and the paint run. I thought, 'much more of this and you will break a thousand ways'.

Maguire were another matter. He was strongly built, high cheekbones and a nose said he fought his share of fisticuffs. He were closer my Papa's age than mine, but he looked good to me and his manner with me were respectful. Dr. had introduced me as Miss Mina Schmidt and Maguire had commented, "Good old country stock." with a nod that made me feel growed a deal more'n I could own.

Soon after, the doll lady woke. I'd learned her name was Josepha. The screaming renewed but I noted not as strong as before. The serving man had told us this was into her second day at it. I understood fully now what Dr. had meant by 'not built for it.'

I stood by her, bathing her forehead, trying to get her to sip sweet, weak herb tea. I learned to dodge her flailing arms mighty quick. She'd lie quiet, groaning soft, then, of a sudden, the screaming and throwing herself would be on us.

Some spare hours before dawn, she started to bleeding... I smelt it first – the sickly sweet odour, a trickle then, just on first light, a river down 'tween her legs. I called the doctor softly.

"Not good, not good..." he stood there a long moment, shaking his head.

She were too weak to more than moan.

Doctor drew Maguire aside and I heard his urgent whisper. "She can't birth the babe. If I take the child by section, she will most like die. If I don't, both will die."

Maguire nodded, "Do best you can."

Josepha never woke from the chloroform. The baby were a boy, swarthy skinned and cleft of chin.

Maguire stepped back, surprise obvious. Then he picked up the first thing to hand, the whiskey bottle and hurled it across the room, smashing it to a million glittering pieces against the stone mantle. The baby whimpered but he paid it no mind.

"WHORE!" he roared the word like judgment day and stormed out. I heard the door slam downstairs and, soon after, horse's hooves pounding the paved carriageway. I wondered at such a display. Not for long - the manservant told us Maguire'd suspected her of an affair with a Confederate officer, Asah Clemens, whilst Maguire was away supplying horses and cattle to the armies. The child had the officer's look, branded with his distinctive cleft.

I thought I understood, the dual trading, that was how Maguire preserved his place. Then I learned more. I learned of the loss of both his grown sons to the War, to opposite sides. He owned no side. My respect for him doubled.

Late in the day, he ambled back, sober but smelling of

whiskey. "Come on doctor, let's have it over with. I've wasted enough on the trollop!"

Josepha was buried without her jewelry, bar a plain band, in the grounds. Her grave marked Josepha Clemens. It were the good doctor's idea. He offered to write to her family in Indiana, Quaker folk, telling of the birth of her boy.

I offered to stay on and care for the child till they came for him, hoping in my heart of hearts to stay much longer than that. This place, for me, were paradise. I were their equal! None of the 'use the servants entrance' Papa and I were so used to with rich folks. I never wanted to leave "Mandolin."

In the days that followed, I made myself useful, not just the babe but round the place. Especially any ways I could make myself helpful to Maguire. He quickly discovered my ability to cipher and my handiness with horses.

Time wore on and the babe prospered. Doctor told me in Maguire's presence, "You're a 'natural,' my girl! You can be right proud! Those Quaker folk ever get here for their grandson, they'll owe you." I blushed. For the first time, it hit me fully, how staying were going to involve me with Maguire - no more as a girl - as a woman. But I weren't a Josepha! No sir, not me!

I fought against needs growing in me I'd seen in the eyes of young runaways, frontier towns I went with Papa. The next year we 'd make it back to a town, sometimes I'd see the same girl again, her eyes different, clothes gaudier. Papa'd shake his head, "Soul gone…" I wanted Maguire's respect and the look as come into his eyes of late, weren't helping none.

One morning, after breakfast, I headed upstairs to check on the babe. Maguire cornered me. His hand barely touched above my elbow, but were lightning through me. I flinched, felt my face flush, "Sir, you surprised me!"

His hand did not move, "Mina, you shall have better."

He wanted to have his dead wife's dressing room for mine but it were too close to his for the sort of relationship I had mind to.

"I need to keep the babe close. The room down end will be right. It has a bay window for his sun kicks," all said, with me looking him straight in the eye and my shoulders back. Maguire said nothing. A glimmer in his eye, told me two things, he didn't like it but he understood. McGinty's shuffling tread behind us, I turned, loosing Maguire's grip. Before I could say aught, Maguire stepped forward, ordering McGinty to help me, "Get the bay room fixed down end, however she wants it!"

Then he turned and looked me up and down more critically, "You're about Jessica, my late wife's fit. Can you sew?"

"Of course! But…"

"I'm beginning to wonder, if there is much you can't do, young woman! Now don't you worry your sweet, young head. My wife would have had it no other way. Jessica was European blood too, you know - Dubonnet." At that point, his shoulders drooped and he looked away. I knew he thought on his twin sons, both sacrificed to this cruel war, the shock too much for poor Jessica.

For me, this were the turning point. I belonged! He'd given me leave to help myself to his late wife's wardrobe! Not my taste, too somber but the addition of some embroidery, a bit of bright ribbon… I truly appreciated the addition to my own scant choice of clothing. But the changes brought a new need for wariness in me, an even greater awareness in Maguire!

The next time Dr. Wilkowski came by to check on the babe, he scarcely recognized me. He leaned in close and whispered, "And I think you've grown a touch. You're quite the lady!" Then he looked me straight in the eye, "Keep it so, Mina."

"Oh yes, Doc!" I felt my cheeks redden. Perhaps he knew my mind. I decided I'd take him into my confidence. I'm glad I did.

Josepha's parents were due in town within the week to collect their grandchild and take their girl's body home. There would be no 'need' for me then and I wanted my part in Mandolin secured.

The day of their arrival, the good doctor came again. He checked the little one over a last time. He would be there to give account of Josepha's last days, were it asked. For what I sensed were entirely different reasons, neither parent wished it.

Straight-laced and grim faced, Mrs Robinson held her grandchild out from her, like some wild and maybe dangerous stray cat she were about to empty out the door. Brother Robinson were very different, fat and jolly and constantly being kicked in the shin for jests he tried to make. She gave me a censorious once over and he it were thanked me for my care of Robert, the name they had settled for the babe. We had prepared a meal for them but she declined and too abruptly to be mistaken.

As we waved them away from our lives, Maguire's arm settled around my shoulders. The good doctor saw it.

I slipped from under Maguire's grasp with a smile and excuse of overseeing McGinty's clumsy ministrations in the kitchen, the cook having taken off with one of the stable hands, a week gone.

Glancing back, I saw Doc guiding Maguire into his own study. As Doc closed the door behind them, he gave me a nod.

That meal together, Doc presiding, marked a whole

difference. Now there were a gentleness in Maguire's look. I fought tears, good ones, the first for a very long time…

I'm standing in the bay window of the nursery, my own babe chuckling and grabbing at sunbeams. Doc has just finished my final examination, post the birth. In the distance, I can hear the merry clanking of pots and pans. Papa is coming to see us. I finger my gold band with its pretty, twinkling diamond and smile, how will I introduce Papa to 'this old goat,' as Maguire called himself, when he asked for my hand? Perhaps the good Doctor will handle that!

J. R. McRae once worked in a circus, as a senior Rare-Books/Reference Librarian, SLQ, as book-reviewer for Department of Education, Qld, as assessment package writer /editor for QSA and Associate Lecturer, English Expression, for international postgraduates, UQ, from which she holds a BA. Her short stories & award winning poetry/haiku are in numerous anthologies & journals, including *Basics of Life* [ALR Anthology], *100 Stories for Queensland, Stories for Sendai, The Spirit of Poe, Trust and Treachery, Poe-it, Wired Ruby and Rose & Thorn, Quadrant, Long and Winding Road, Bound by the Secrets We Hide, Antipodes, Social Alternatives.* Her Artwork/photography features in Musings: A Mosaic, Colours of Refuge, *Ripples, ABC Pool, The Mozzie* and *Vine Leaves.* As multi-award winning children's writer, J.R.Poulter, she has over 30 books for children & education published and over 30 digital picture books. More print books are coming.
Websites: http://www.jrmcrae_subversive.weebly.com,
http://www.jenniferrpoulter.weebly.com/

Terry Hand has had a long and varied career in almost all areas of illustration. He has exhibited prints at the Royal Academy Summer Exhibition and The Royal Society for Painter Etchers. He lives in London.
http://terryhand.blogspot.co.uk

Acknowledgement of Prior Publication

Each of the four interlinking stories in FREE PASSAGE was previously published in an anthology or journal.

A House Divided in *Basics of Life*, Australian Literature Review anthology, edited by Steve Rossiter, 2011

Girl's Story in both *Wordgathering* (Australia), Dec 2014 & *Kaleidoscope* (USA), issue 71, 2015

The Making of Me in *A Journey You Say?*, editor, Chris Bartholomew, Static Movement Press, Georgia, USA, 2013

Mina in A *Journey You Say?*, editor, Chris Bartholomew, Static Movement Press, Georgia, USA, 2013

www.ingramcontent.com/pod-product-compliance
Lightning Source LLC
Chambersburg PA
CBHW070805120626
46557CB00002B/722
* 9 7 8 1 9 2 5 4 8 4 1 1 3 *